RULER OF THE COURTYARD

by RUKHSANA KHAN

Illustrated by R. GREGORY CHRISTIE

Viking

VIKING

Published by the Penguin Group

Penguin Putnam Books for Young Readers, 345 Hudson Street, New York, New York 10014, U.S.A.

Penguin Books Ltd, 80 Strand, London WC2R 0RL, England

Penguin Books Australia Ltd, 250 Camberwell Road, Camberwell, Victoria 3124, Australia

Penguin Books Canada Ltd, 10 Alcorn Avenue, Toronto, Ontario, Canada M4V 3B2

Penguin Books (N.Z.) Ltd, 182-190 Wairau Road, Auckland 10, New Zealand

Penguin Books Ltd, Registered Offices: Harmondsworth, Middlesex, England

First published in 2003 by Viking, a division of Penguin Putnam Books for Young Readers.

1 3 5 7 9 10 8 6 4 2

Text copyright © Rukhsana Khan, 2003
Illustrations copyright © R. Gregory Christie, 2003

MAR 2 7 2003

LIBRARY OF CONGRESS CATALOGING-IN-PUBLICATION DATA
Khan, Rukhsana, date-
Ruler of the courtyard / by Rukhsana Khan ; illustrated by R. Gregory Christie. p. cm.
Summary: After confronting what she believes to be a snake in the bath house,
Saba finds the courage to overcome her fear of the chickens in the courtyard.
ISBN 0-670-03583-1
[1. Fear—Fiction. 2. Pakistan—Fiction.] I. Christie, Gregory, date-, ill. II. Title.
PZ7.K52654Ru 2003   [E]—dc21   2002010167

Manufactured in China
Set in Adrift
Book design by Nancy Brennan

The art was rendered in acrylics on illustration board with a palette knife.

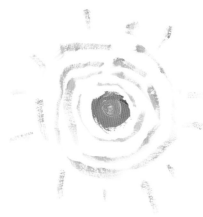

For my mother, Iftikhar Shahzadi Khan, and my sister-in-law,

Yusra Khan, who each inspired part of this story.—**R.K.**

For Aslam N. Chaudhry and Kirn Chaudhry. I did my best to honor your

lesson. I hope that the children in both regions attain their bravery and

understanding during these times of conflict.—**R.G.C.**

hickens, big and small, seem to have a certain know-it-all knack for sensing when I'm feeling scared. I can't remember when I had no fear of them. They've been the very terror of my life.

Bony beaks, razor claws, with GLITTERY eyes that wonder,
wonder as they watch me, how easy it would be to make me scream.

SQUEAK, the door swings open.

I peek in both directions.

The way is clear, not a bird in sight.

Dash to the bathhouse.

Out of nowhere they come running.

It seems I haven't got a right to cross the courtyard.

SLAM the bathhouse door.

Inside, it's safe and quiet. Scratching at the dirt, they wait eagerly nearby. They must know I have to leave sometime.

Fill the bucket, find the soap, wash my hair, and lather up. Forget the terrors lingering outside.

Rinse well and I am done. Towel dry and dress. Sit upon the bench and comb my hair.

How peaceful and silent it is inside the bathhouse.
How dim and calm and cool. I take my time.
Then I spy a curled-up something in the corner. How
did I miss it? Within easy striking distance of the door.

It's brownish black. Is it moving? Is it HISSING?
Is it watching? Waiting till I'm close enough to bite?

I want to scream, but if I do, Nani will come running.

Footsteps.

Heavy POUNDING.

Alarming coils of danger on the floor.

She'll come BURSTING, without knowing,
through the door.

It could bite. She could die.

So I swallow up the scream inside and slowly, very
slowly, I stand upon my feet.

A WEAPON! I need a weapon to kill the deadly snake! With one eye on the corner, I search and find a stick—long and hard enough to do the job.

I can't do it. Just can't do it. Can't bring myself to kill it, and yet it has to go. It cannot stay!

A TRAP. Oh yes a trap! With a trap I could get rid of it. A trap would save us all from the venom of the snake.

But what to use? Something deep, something hard the snake can't bite through. Something like a cover, something like a pot.

What about the bucket?

It's perfect for the purpose, so I grip the handles tight, so firmly that my knuckles turn to white.

But how can I go closer? I only want to run and look for cover! Go anywhere but closer to the danger in the corner by the door.

There's no choice.

None at all.

No one else is here to do it.

I HAVE to trap the snake. Forget about my fear.

STEP.

Then again.

Like a puppet on a string.

Make my feet take me closer. Don't think of where I'm going. And while I'm at it, don't forget to breathe.

Trap it on the first try. Might not get another. Tighten up my courage. Open up my eyes. HERE IT GOES!

Did I do it? Did I catch it? Peeking through my fingers, I look to see what happened to the snake.

I missed.

PRESSED against the wall, I strain to reach the bucket.
Is it coiling up to strike? Or moving back to leave?
I hear it hiss and slither, scales rubbing one another.
Or is it just the rushing of my breath?

Every hair is standing, all along my spine. I'm shaking but
determined. I cannot fail again. Very very carefully, when the
time is right, I slam the bucket down around the snake.

All is silent. All is still.

Not a movement, not a rustle.

I can't believe I did it.

I can breathe.

But it's too quiet, much too quiet. No sound's coming from the bucket. No moving or hissing of a trapped and angry snake. Did I somehow kill it after all?

A moment passes. Then another. And another. And one more. Still absolutely silent, I'm waiting for a sign the snake's ALIVE.

I can't STAND it any longer. I must know if I have killed it. With the stick, I lift the bucket up.

I blink.

I can't BELIEVE it.

It's not a snake at all.

It's a drawstring. A nala. I trapped my Nani's nala. All that fuss to catch the rope that ties up Nani's baggy pants.

Then I'm LAUGHING really hard. I cannot seem to stop. It's
such a great relief. Better, so much better, than my fear.

When my laughter quiets and my sides have finished aching, I
gather up the bath things, take my Nani's nala, and open up the door.
The chickens are still waiting. SQUAWKING, screeching. They
jump at me and try to peck my toes.

From deep within me comes a ROAR.

I giggle when they scatter. They're shrieking.
Have they lost their little minds?

Did the chickens really scare me? It seems so long
ago. They're savage little bullies, nothing more.

To be a little wicked, taste the honey of revenge, I
drop my things so I can CHASE the chickens.

Through many feathers flying, I run laughing, I run shouting, "I AM MIGHTY SABA! RULER OF THE COURTYARD!" No more will I stay cooped up in the house.

And now the chickens know I've got a right to cross the courtyard and walk wherever I may wish to go.